KARADI TALES

Nandini Nayar
Francesco Manetti

What Will You Give Me?

'I am bored,' Sameer said.

Amma smiled. 'I have just the thing!' she said.
And do you know what she did? She told him a story.

Also available in the
Curious Sameer
Series:

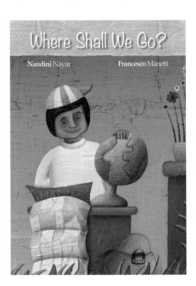

What Will You Give Me?

For Pramod and Pranav
— Nandini Nayar

Author: Nandini Nayar
Illustrator: Francesco Manetti

Karadi Tales Company Pvt. Ltd.
3A Dev Regency 11 First Main Road Gandhinagar Adyar Chennai 600020
Ph: +91 44 4205 4243 Email: contact@karaditales.com
Website: www.karaditales.com

Distributed in North America by Consortium Book Sales & Distribution
The Keg House 34 Thirteenth Avenue NE Suite 101 Minneapolis MN 55413-1006 USA
Orders: (+1) 731-423-1550; orderentry@perseusbooks.com
Electronic ordering via PUBNET (SAN 631760X); Website: www.cbsd.com

Printed in India
ISBN No.: 978-81-8190-286-3

'I give up!' Amma said, 'What do you want me to give you?'

'I want you to give me something that will help me fly like the bird and soar like the kite, sail like the boat and steer like the captain, I want to see the whole world and wear a sailor's hat and a garland of flowers! Can you give me something that will help me do all that?'

'Then I will give you some cardboard,'
Amma said.

'If you give me cardboard,' Sameer
said, 'I will make a strong box so that
the boy can keep his things safe in it.'

'Then what will you give me?'

'Shall I give you a sheet of paper?' Amma said.

'If you give me a sheet of paper,' Sameer said, 'I will fold it and bend it. I will pull it and pat it. And I will make a beautiful boat with it. Then I will sail it in the water. The boat will go faster and faster and sail far away!'

'Then what will you give me?'

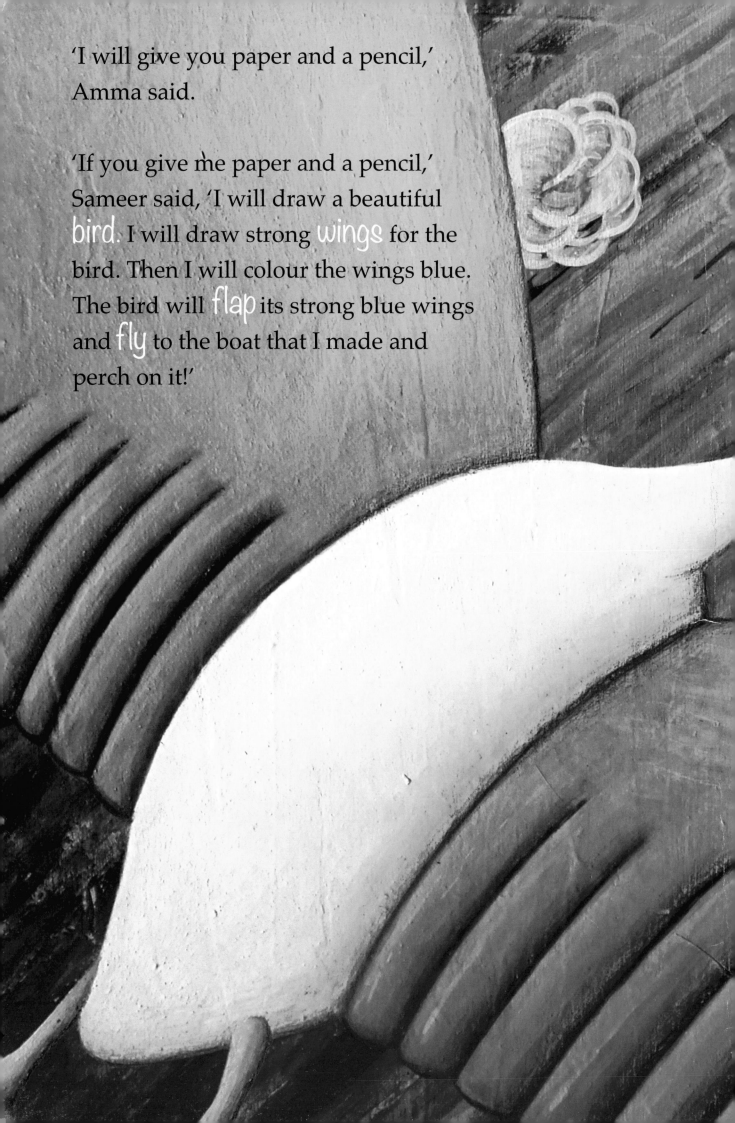

'I will give you paper and a pencil,'
Amma said.

'If you give me paper and a pencil,'
Sameer said, 'I will draw a beautiful
bird. I will draw strong wings for the
bird. Then I will colour the wings blue.
The bird will flap its strong blue wings
and fly to the boat that I made and
perch on it!'

'Then what will **you** give me?'

'Then I will give you paper and string,' Sameer's mother said.

'If you give me paper and string,' Sameer said, 'I will make a kite with a long tail. Then I will tie the string to it and fly it high in the sky. The wind will take the kite far away! The kite will fly over the bird with the blue wings, perched on the boat that I made.'

'Then what will you give me?'

'Then I will give you some clay,' Amma said.

'If you give me clay,' Sameer said, 'I will make a little boy with two hands, two legs, a head, a nose, two ears and one mouth. The boy will sail the boat into the distant seas!'

'Then what will you give me?'

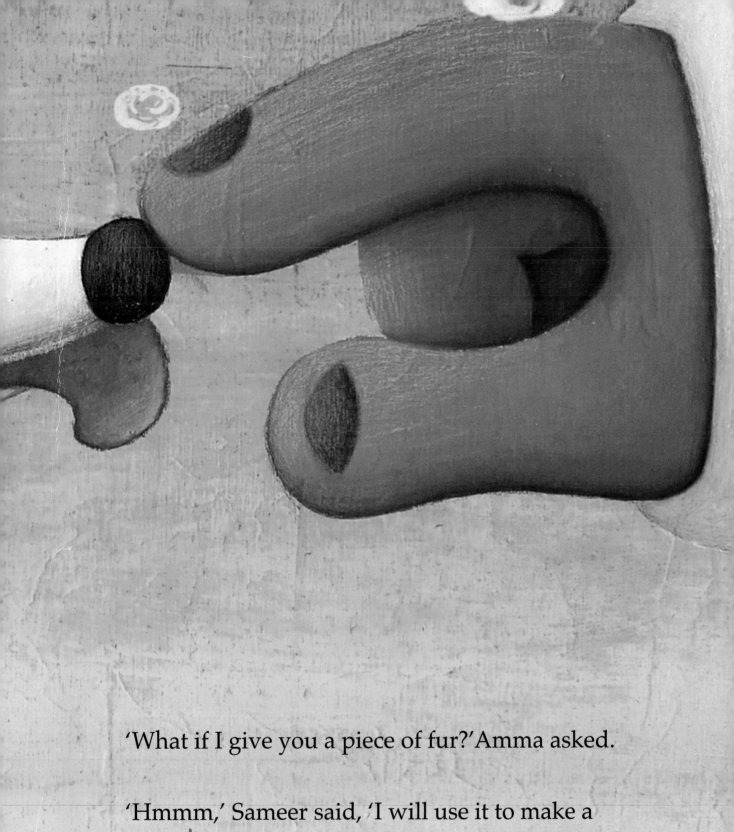

'What if I give you a piece of fur?' Amma asked.

'Hmmm,' Sameer said, 'I will use it to make a little dog with a curly little tail and a happy smile to be the boy's best friend!'

'Then what will you give me?'

'Then I will give you some sticks,' Amma said.

'If you give me sticks,' Sameer said, 'I will build a little house for the dog. The dog will sit in the house when he is tired of sailing with the boy into the distant seas.'

'Then **what** will you give me?'

'Then I will give you paper and scissors,' Amma said.

'If you give me paper and scissors,' Sameer said, 'I will cut out beautiful flowers for the boy to wear as he sails the boat.'

'What will you give me then?'

'I will give you some cloth,' Amma said.

'If you give me cloth,' Sameer said, 'I will make a sailor's hat for the boy and he'll wear it and call himself Captain.'

'What will you give me then?'

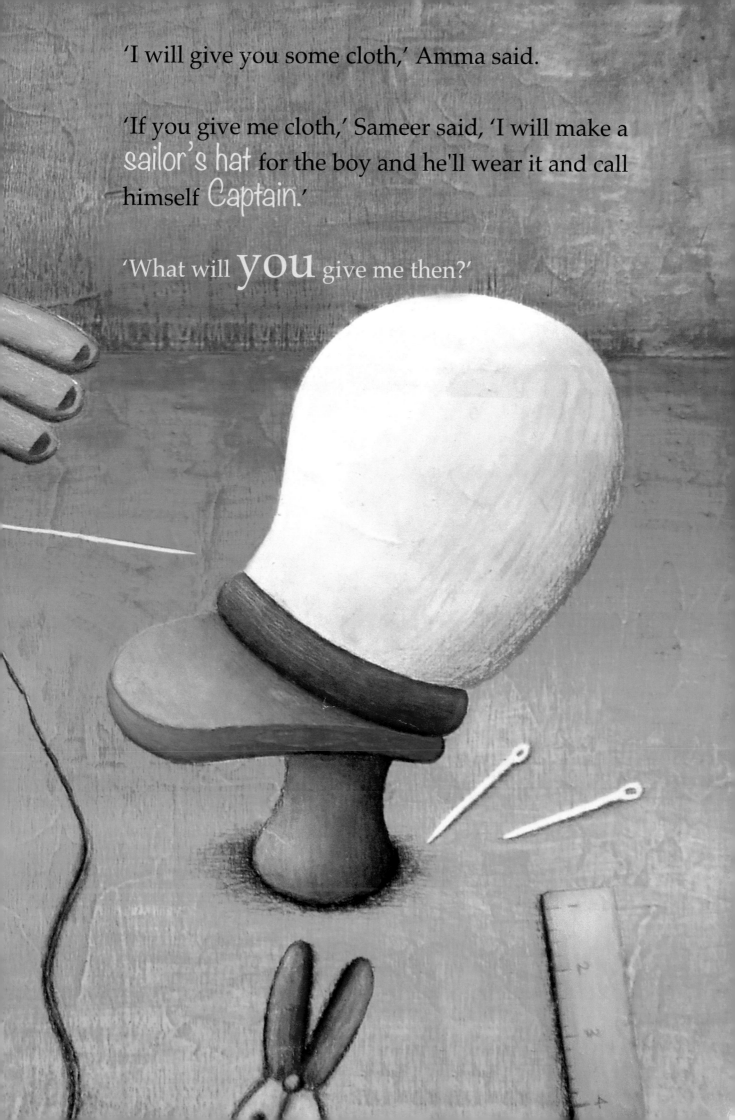

'Then I will give you needle and thread,' Amma said.

'If you give me needle and thread,' Sameer said, 'I will stitch a big C on the boy's hat so that everyone will know he is the captain when he sails the boat into the distant seas.'

'Then what will you give me?'